Bergen Weeks Applegate

Poems and Ballads

Bergen Weeks Applegate

Poems and Ballads

ISBN/EAN: 9783337374921

Printed in Europe, USA, Canada, Australia, Japan

Cover: Foto ©Andreas Hilbeck / pixelio.de

More available books at **www.hansebooks.com**

Poems

AND

Ballads.

-BY-

Bergen Weeks Applegate.

DELPHI, IND
Printed at the Journal Office.
1885.

NOTE.

THIS edition is limited to one hundred copies, of which this copy is No. .7. The author desires to express his thanks to those who so generously subscribed for his work; through whose encouragement, and in many instances personal aid, its publication became possible.

PREFACE.

THE poems in this little collection, were for the most part, written during my school days; and, with the exception of four, while still in my teens. Of them, I know naught that I may say, prefatory, more appropriate than quote the sentiment which Swinburne so delicately expresses in a dedication :

"Some sang to me dreaming in class-time,
    And truant in hand as in tongue ;
For the youngest were born of boy's pastime,
    The eldest are young."

While it is highly probable, that, at the best, these poems can be but short lived, saving, perhaps, in the consideration of intimate friends; may I not, unpresumingly, say of this early Muse, as did Keats on a similar occasion, that, although "a sad thought for me," I have "some hope that while it is dwindling I may be plotting and fitting myself for verses fit to live."   B. W. A.

DELPHI, Aug. 29, 1885.

DEDICATION.

Take these poor songs of mine, Maiden,
  To thee, and none else, they belong;
For thou wert their birth in their weakness, Maiden,
  Thou only may lift them up strong.
Some faltering melodies, Maiden,
  Charm with echoes, sweet music long dead;
I am paid having caught but the cadence
  From the songs that the master hearts fed.

Take these poor songs of mine, Maiden,
  Thou will nurse what a world would destroy;
Weeds, grasses, and rain-beaten blossoms,
  Culled by the hands of a boy.
Frail as they are to behold, Maiden,
  Little worth in the world's busy mart;
Take, O! take them, they budded sincerely
  From the pulse of a passionate heart.

CONTENTS.

Tempus vernum flores suos primos fragiles habet.

POEMS AND BALLADS

THE DREAM-PILLOW.

Dreams are true while they last,
  And do we not live in dreams?
      —*Tennyson.*

I.

THERE came a sailor up from the sea,
Many a wonderful tale told he.

Tales of idols with emerald eyes ;
Of dusky maidens and Indian skies ;

Tales of robbers and bandits free :
And pirates that sailed the tropic sea ;

Legends learned in the land of Bael ;
From swarthy Brahmins in Cashmere vale :

Of witches and brownies, faeries and elves,
And the mermaid queen in her palace of shells :

Tales of the marvellous land of the East,
Where the sun is god, and the moon high priest.

II.

The village folk, both young and old,
Came out to hear the tales he told.

And with them, fairest one of three,
Came timid, dark-eyed Margery.

Fair as a sea-flower, lithe and tall—
Clinging alone to the old sea wall.

The sailor's wave-lit, mild, gray eyes
Twinkled like stars in the evening skies.

For of all his sweethearts over the sea,
There was none so fair as Margery ;

And the sailor lost his heart, I'm told,
For all he was sun-browned, withered and old.

III.

Yet a right warm heart the sailor had,
And he was gallant as any lad.

So he wooed the maiden still and shy,
With the foam-white face and dark blue eye.

But his suit was vain and it grieved him sore,
Till he wished himself leagues from the Cor-
	nish shore.

But ere he followed his messmates gay,
Down to the ship to sail away.

He paused to open his treasured store,
And a costly gift to the maiden bore ;

The dream-pillow at her feet he laid,
Bade her farewell, nor longer stayed.

IV.

Fair Margery smiled as she looked to see
The sailor's magical legacy.

Yet the shining pillow, soft as down,
Was a valued gift and of great renown.

Long it had lain in a temple grand—
The richest prize of a heathen land.

'Twas filled with poppies and lotus bloom,
And strange sweet herbs with soft perfume.

And this was the legend writ in gold
Across the blue of its silken fold :

*Who slumbers here with conscience free
Give I the visions asked of me.*

V.

When twilight fell with shadows gray.
Pure Margery knelt down to pray.

And ere her blue eyes lost the light,
Wished for a dream of angels bright.

When the white mist began to creep
Athwart the sands, she feel asleep.

She dreamed she stood at a pearly gate
The night was stormy, the hour was late ;

But the great bars fell, and the hinges turned,
And a gold light into the darkness burned ;

And a sweet incense of flower and spice
Swept the colonnades of Paradise.

VI.

The fairest of an angel band
She wandered through the summer land.

To tell her visions I would fain,
But words blow off like mist from rain.

The wondrous dreams she had each night,
Filled her blue eyes with strange delight.

And when she told her sisters two
The wonder o'er the village flew.

And from the village inn, 'tis said,
The tidings o'er the kingdom spread ;

Until the courtiers did convene
And posted off to tell the Queen.

VII.

When the great Queen had heard the tale
She bade her knights go arm and mail.

An hundred gallants at her side,
For nights and days she then did ride ;

And when they halted by the sea
She sought the sailor's legacy.

And gentle Margery, modest maid,
At the Queen's feet her treasure laid.

The Queen bore off the prize that night
And wished for dreams of wealth and might.

She dreamed her realm had passed away.
And woke in wrath at break of day.

VII.

Down to the sea she rode in haste,
And cast the treasure on the waste.

From her poor cot sad Margery wept
To see her pillow outward swept;

And when the Queen, superb and grand.
Rode off. she hastened to the strand :

She sadly searched the dunes and drift,
But nowhere found the magic gift.

When from the sea the round moon leapt.
Upon the sand she lay and wept.

And there her sisters, scared and white.
Found her slumbering far in the night.

IX.

They bore her homeward, still asleep.
O'er sands and crags wave-washed and steep.

And when she woke. late in the morn.
Poor Margery looked quite forlorn.

For days and days o'er the bright sea
Her dark blue eyes fell wistfully.

But the magic pillow had drifted far.
And never came in o'er the harbor bar.

Perhaps. thro' Chance's quaint design.
It lay once more on its Eastern shrine.

*   *   *   *   *   *   *   *   *

And winds and waves made sad refrain
Where the tar went down on the Spanish Main.

THE BIRTH OF THE YEAR.

THE chancel lamp burned dim and low
　　We stood beside the frosted pane ;
　　The moon shone on the burnished vane,
And silence kissed the virgin snow.

The shadows played the aisles among,
　　Or lingered ghost-like in the pews,
　　Or launched their spirit-barks to cruise
The holy walls with holly hung.

The village folk their converse kept
　　In accents hushed, and sounding strange
　　As each soft echo took her range
And bathed the cross by angels wept.

She leaned her cheek upon her hand ;
　　Her eyes were deep with truth and love.
　　The clock ticked gaily up above--
The old year waited on the strand.

One finger raised she to her lip --
　　The clock above began to chime.
　　A youth strode down in rosy prime
And led the old man to the ship.

THE MILLER.

O, a song of the genial miller,
  How I envy the life he leads!
And I hear in the hum of the grinding,
  The praise of his days and deeds.

A mile from the town the mill is:
  A lane leads off to the left;
And there half hid in the foliage,
  It lies at the foot of a cleft.

A brooklet runs at the doorway,
  But the mill pond lies o'erhead
In the meadow upon the height,
  With many a lily spread.

And its waters, how they ripple
  Down over the moss-green wheel,
With a tinkle of sharp, clear echoes
  Ringing a merry reel!

While the weary wheel, slow turning
  To the sound of the music sweet,
Sighs, an old man treading a measure
  'Mid younger and livelier feet.

I tied my horse at the hitching block,
    And mounted the five-step stair;
The miller grasped my hand at the door—
    He was jolly as he was fair.

The month was June, and the morning sun
    Shot one bright ray on the clean white floor;
As together we sat—the miller and I—
    On the bench at the open door.

We talked of the weather—the growing corn—
    The harvesting that was near at hand;
Of trade, and commerce, and social strife;
    Of travel by sea and land.

We talked of England, the land of his birth:
    And he told gay tales of the merry time
When he was a boy, with a boy's wild will,
    When life with love made a mellow rhyme.

Of the old wind-mill his father owned,
    A mile from York, to the east;
How it seemed at dusk with its great wings
       spread,
    Some terrible being, half bird, half beast.

And his good wife came to us there at the door,
    Smiling sweet thro' her gold-rimmed glasses,
As she told of her home on the river Dart,
    Of Yorkshire lads and Devon lasses.

Of her noble daughter—how one spring night
  When the swollen pond burst over the hill,
Thro' the beating storm to the town she sped
  For aid, and saved the mill.

And my friend the miller and I sat there,
  While the great wheel, muttering low,
Kept count of the hours as they came and went,
  With a measured beat and slow.

Till the sun stood over the slanting roof,
  And we heard his daughter cry
That the sacks were running over,
  And the hopper had run dry.

c

MY LOVE JEAN.

WHAT though the cabin be old, Jean,
  And the moss-green thatch decayed ;
The roses are over the window, Jean,
  And the door-yard dark with shade ;
And your garden's ablaze with bloom, Jean,
  It burns for the sun and for you ;
The grass is soft to your bare feet, Jean,
  They are white and your gown is blue.

Out here in the wild, red West, Jean.
  A heath-bell blown far overseas ;
You're the fairest that ever hath wandered,
    Jean,
  From the green of Caledonian leas ;
And there are warm hearts in the West, Jean,
  We love you as we love our own ;
Though we falter and stutter our songs, Jean.
  'Tis the soul of the song that is known.

What though labor be irksome at noon, Jean,
  Toilers only are blessed with sweet rest ;

And the low log hut by the woodside, Jean,
   No thrush ever had such a nest;
'Twas there in the gloom I first saw you, Jean,
   By the well where the alders were white;
And silent, and thoughtful, you come to me
     oft, Jean,
   In day dreams and dreams of the night.

AT VESPER HOUR.

At vesper hour she knelt to pray
Within the cloister dusk and gray.
   Mary, the Mother, smiled on her ;
   Sweet the voice of the chorister
Chanted the solemn hour away.

This was her prayer :   Be thou my stay.
O Virgin fair !   O Christ !   I stray ;
   Lift me from sin, I faint, I err.
            At vesper hour.

An angel at the gates of Day
Heard the low voice ; in bright array
   Came, an heavenly messenger ;
   Knelt by the holy sepulchre ;
And two souls prayed where one did pray.
            At vesper hour.

FAERY-LAND.

IN AN ALBUM.

'Tis but a step to Faery-land,
  'Tis just behind yon sloping hill;
There are some who found it long ago,
  And some who seek it still.
A genie guards the gateway,
  O, his heart is large and warm;
'Tis he who opens the portals,
  He keeps out every harm.

This world is that magical faery-land;
  'Tis a faery-land to him
Who, thro' trouble, and care, and storm,
  Sees over the rainbow's rim.
The soul is that genie guard—
  Kind words, kind deeds, light heart,
And he beckons us gently forward,
  Whilst the portals swing apart.

SONNET.

[Written after having listened to ANNA DICKINSON deliver her lecture on JOAN of Arc.]

Ah me! Joan of Arc, bright saint above,
    'Mid angel hosts; crowned with the victor's
        wreath,
    Thy banner dust, thy sword hid in the
        sheath,
Thy battles o'er! At last, O, wounded dove,
At rest within the realm where all is love!
    Didst thou not hear the voice that spake
        thy name?
That told how for thy country's good thou
        strove.
    Yet held thy love of God above all fame?
Surely its echoes touched thy listening ear,
    Borne on the airy waves from this far land,
Surely, methinks, thy gentle soul didst hear
    Its music break upon the golden strand,
And thrill in answer to the love it bore
From thy fair sister of the earthly shore.

A TRIAD OF SONNETS.

FROM, *The Odors:* A FABLE IN SONNET.

*   *   *   *   *   *   *

I.

I AM the odor of full blown roses.
    Without me would the air of leafy June
      Grow lonely, and the thrush her sweet
        voice tune
To a low sad plaint ; for where reposes
In gardens, or faery-haunted closes,
      The soul of me, there is Queen Summer's
        breath
Said to fall sweetest, and there imposes
    On the mortal heart, raptures kin to death.

When time goes on and my sweet parents die —
    Sad shorn of all their grace by wandering air :
Then doth the season's essence seem to fly,
    And beauty die with their strewn petals fair.

Then am I wafted over heaven's wall,
Obedient to an angel's beckoning call.

II.

I am the odor of hay, newly mown.
    I come from meadows girt with hedges
        green.
    Set 'round with alders white, and in be-
        tween,
Pink briar roses, wet with clear dew thrown
By angel hands from cups of ruby-stone.
    I am the soul of waving grasses tall;
All earth is my one heaven. I alone
    Am rightfully queen odor over all.

My breath keeps fresh a thousand tender lays,
    Carolled by birds and many a lovely maid;
What happy thoughts of long dead summer
        days
    I call from out the past's sequestered
        shade.

He who hath felt my breath upon his cheek,
Pauseth, nor yet a sweeter deigns to seek.

III.

I am the odor of tall, ripening wheat.
    Ebbing in golden waves at hush of noon;
    Waiting the scythe and harvest songs of
        June.

I am the rarest of all odors sweet.
Making the heart of him, whose bruised feet
    Bled at the sowing time, to take good heed,
And in the fullness of his soul repeat:
    They who aweary sow, shall reap indeed.

I tell a tale of hunger satisfied;
    The poor man blesses me as Christ did
        bless
Ere He on Calvary's mount was crucified.
    The tales I tell are all of happiness.

On earth shall I remain, from heaven sent,
The soul of the most sacred sacrament.

*   *   *   *   *   *   *

ODE TO SILVANUS.

FOR AN ARBOR DAY CELEBRATION.

[In Roman mythology, Silvanus is the god of the forest. He is represented as an old man scattering flowers, and usually bears in his hand a pruning-knife.]

'Twas thro' a music-haunted grove,
  Greened by the regal sun ;
Where sacred Faunus loved to rove
  And pipe when day was done:
A bard—fond lover of the forest dews—
Wandered at eve, to court the gentle Muse.

As thro' the balmy perfumed air.
Adown a vista fresh and rare.
  Bright in the sun's last ray,
He wandered ; wading thro' the bloom
Young Spring had scattered o'er the tomb
  Of Winter, old and gray ;
There chanced before his roving eye.
Far off, but slowly drawing nigh.

A figure, strange as ere was seen,
All clad in flowing robes of green.

In mute surprise the bard stood still.
  Ah, well. full well, he might!
And thro' his soul there went a thrill
  Awakened at the sight.
Silvanus! Rome's most favored god!
God of the forest. staunch and old ;
God of the flowerets. blue and gold,
Seen only by the solemn priest,
And augur gray at silvan feast,
  And consecrated sacrifice.
Or. now and then, some mighty bard.
  Whose soaring fancies run
The round of worlds, roam thro' the moon.
  And gardens of the sun.

In wonder wrapped, amid the bloom
That seemed to daunt the gath'ring gloom.
  The bard in reverence stood;
And watched the old man totter nigh ;
And heard his voice that seemed a sigh
  Of branches of the wood ;
And saw him strew along the way,
Like stolen star-beams, gleaming, gay.
  His garlands rare and grand ;

And listened to the song that rose.
And swelled, and died, in soft repose.
Before his beck'ning hand :

> " I scatter here, I scatter there,
> By brooklet clear, by fountain fair,
> O'er sloping plain, o'er mountain high.
> By raging main, by desert dry.
> O mortal man !   List to my lay !
> Thy life can span but one brief day ;
> Then why deface, is my one plea.
> The lovely race I've reared for thee ? "

To which the bard :
" O, aged father of a mighty race !
A world doth bow before thy verdant throne !
Thy sturdy folds adore thy matchless face.
    And lift their praise on high from zone to
        zone !
O, mighty ruler of a boundless realm
    That stretches far to Neptune's blue domain.
Without thee, could frail mortal guide the helm
    Of State, or e'en his shadowed life maintain?
How may he, who would court thy grace—
    Who would thy servant be——"

And as the sighing winds that trace
　The sobbing, billowed sea:—

　　"I scatter here, I scatter there—
　　O Man, give ear!　O Man, beware!
　　Lift not thine arm in maddened haste,
　　My realm to harm with wanton waste!
　　O, let it live—to thrive—increase!
　　To thee 'twill give undying peace.
　　As swift as bird flies o'er the lea,
　　My wrath incurred shall follow thee."

"O, thou, thrice blessed god, who reared on
　　Earth,
　To share with erring Man, thy blest abode;
To cheer a world that else were fraught with
　　dearth,
　To wake the fount of Love that ne'er had
　　flowed!
O, thou, to whom, when fraught with grief
　　and pain—
When Melancholy's sable pall hangs low—
Mankind may turn, and at thy smile regain
　A rest, a peace, unsullied by the glow that
　　gleams from proud Ambition!
O, thou, creator of the leafy cell,

And shaded glen where perfumed zephyrs
  blow.
Where happy Satyrs, frisking. love to tell
  Their secrets, and their tearful tales of woe!
Where Orpheus learned to twang his magic
  lyre.
  And move the stony hearts to beat with
  life ;
Where still the notes shall cling and ne'er
  expire.
  Though ages roll and surge with maddened
  strife !
O. parent of the laurel and the pine.
  Beneath whose shade the Dryads love to
  rove.
Where bards inspired, breath forth the mighty
  line
  That reaches to the throne of high-born Jove!
  How may the world repay——"

But darkness hid the form from view,
  And all alone the bard stood still ;
A star fell from the vaulted blue;
  The crescent moon sank 'neath the hill.
And in the sighing of the breeze

He seemed to hear, as o'er the trees
    It swept in haste along:—

  "I scatter here, I scatter there,
O Man, give ear! O Man, beware!
I rear for thee my temples grand;
From sea to sea I deck the land:
For thee and thine, I sow, I reap;
Yet all is mine—thy trust well keep.
Swift as a bird flies o'er the lea,
My wrath incurred shall follow thee."

THE FARMER'S LAMENT.

No, I ain't the feller I used to be
'Way back in the summer o' 'Forty-three,
When I was a strappin' farmer lad
From head to foot in homespun clad;
When I plowed, an' planted, an' grubbed, an'
  .   hoed,
On that old farm yender, acrost the road;
When I was the stoutest feller around,
An' weighed nigh on two hundred pound,
An' at gittin' away with a good square meal,
Could beat an ox in a clover fiel'.
But all them things has slipped from me.
An' I ain't the feller I used to be.

No, I ain't the feller I used to be
When I was a youngster in 'Forty-three;
My back is humped, an' my hair is gray,

An' my appetite's clean died away :
My eyes is dim, an' my steps is slow.
Fer the years has got my frame in tow.
But they're pullin' me on a most too fast.
An' I'm feared they'll pull me down at last.
Fer I ain't the heart to fight 'em now.
With this fearful weight upon my brow :
An' all the people a-sayin' to me :
"You ain't the feller you used to be."

No. I ain't the feller I used to be.
When I was a-farmin' in 'Forty-three :
When I got up early in the morn
An' mowed the hay, an' shucked the corn:
An' hunted fer eggs in the old barn loft.
'Mid the timothy hay an' clover soft ;
An' the apples shook in the early fall.
An' stored 'em away fer a "future call ;"
An' tramped along each wintry day
To the old log school house acrost the way.
Little dreamin' I ever the day would see
When I'd wish I'as the feller I used to be.

No. I ain't the feller I used to be
When I was young in 'Forty-three.
This world fer me ain't got no charm.

Fer a dry old town ain't like a farm :
An' there ain't a face on this earth I know
Like mother's, who died long years ago ;
An' I ain't a friend since father's gone,
That I kin trust or lean upon.
But they're waitin' fer me in that land so fair
An' I trust when I die I shall journey there ;
An' I think I'll git in, thro' God's decree,
Though I *ain't* the feller I used to be.

FRAGMENTS OF A STUDY.

HER full, sweet throat is curved as a calla's,
    yet much whiter,
  And where it leans o'er languid layers of
    lace, and brooch of pearl-flower.
No silver chalice out from purple altar-cloth
    shone brighter,
  No white flower was there bloomed so fair
    in Eden's heavenly bower.

Her eyes, such wealth of color therein dwells,
    that but to name
  Would tax the wit of many master painters,
    who in pure dreams
See all Paradise in bounteous bloom. Bernardo
    saw the same
  Ere from the soul of Beatrice the grief-
    spring ran in streams.

*   *   *   *   *   *   *

Oftimes, day-dreaming, have I fancied that
    amethyst in wine,
  Clear amethyst like unto April skies, in
    wine blood red.
Held that one hue, that deep, dark shade,
    half earthly, half divine.
  Ah, me! what hosts of pale spring blossoms
    thereon might be fed.

From breast to brow there is not one red spot
    — all there is white,
  Save when to some sweet shame or sudden
    fright, the crimson tide
Deep flushes throat, and cheeks, and trembling
    temples bright.
  Leaving in its slow ebbing purer what it
    deigned to hide.

Some there were who said her blood was half
    alien; and that her face
  Betrayed the evil secret of her birth: most
    knowingly
Their wise heads shook, as though 'twas that
    which any fool might trace.
  Mary of Nazareth had the same; and it was
    heavenly!

*   *   *   *   *   *   *

Yet. with that hour, my love it grew apace. for
her pure soul
Was purer than her face was bright; and
if, perchance, I err
And strike the lyre too sharply, bringing wild
notes where soft should roll.
Forgive, my heart hath over-leapt itself for
love of her.

EDGAR ALLAN POE.

O POET! thou whose errant fancies wild,
    Didst wander far from Earth's broad fields
        of light.
    To roam amidst the realms of boundless
        night :
Sad and alone, like some unguided child,
By faery's spell or genie's charm beguiled.
    O thou! whose heart Misfortune's cruel hand
Chilled ere the flowers of love had oped and
        smiled,
    Or glowed the fires affection might have
        fanned.

Hadst not within thy path the early grave
    Oped to receive thee in thy manhood's
        prime :
Hadst but the world put forth a hand to save,
    Who knows what heights thy spirit might
        in time
Have mounted ? Who—who knows but that
        thy name
To-day might shine first on the scroll of fame?

THE CHILD AND THE PICTURE.

A LITTLE maid she was, blue-eyed and fair.
  A tender bud with simple childish ways ;
Too young to know of life and seasons sad,
    Of doubt, or dread of death, for childhood
        days
Are those beyond the realm of vaulted sky—
Bright angel days where pleasures multiply.

She had her loving mother's pensive face;
  Golden her hair was, like silk in yellow skein;
Four times had wild flowers decked the robes
    of May.
    And summer suns four times had riped
      the grain,
Since her blue orbs, at Heaven's wise decree,
First oped to life and all its mystery.

Ah me! what love there was between the two—
  Between the mother and the fair-haired
    child :
Men marvelled at two souls so closely wove,

For earth-born love is wayward, weak and
    wild.
I doubt not that the love they two were given
Was least of earth and nearest that of Heaven.

Alas! One day the pale Destroyer came,
    And with the still-faced parent gently
        clasped
Close in his arms, wept o'er the lonely child,
    Then winged his flight to the far land of rest,
Leaving the lonely one in wonderment and
        tears,
Her tender heart abeat with growing fears.

As the slow hours went on and one day fled,
    And o'er the low west meads the twilight
        fell,
The wistful eyes broke tears ; and comfortless,
    She wept most piteously ; and the swell
Of great grief bursting, none were there could
        stay ;
E'en the old nurse looked on with sad dismay.

And still the child, with each slow dying day,
    Cried and cried. and they but wasted breath
Who deigned to comfort her ; for hour by hour

Her tears fell fresh. till she came nigh to
    death,
Yet no sweet comfort came. and they around
Shook their heads sadly to hear the mournful
    sound.

One day. at eve, the old nurse wandered out.
    Bearing the child with her across the way;
Under the gray cathedral walls they paused—
    A sweet-faced nun came there at dusk to
      pray.
She marked the careworn nurse—the child in
    tears,
And gently reaching out she soothed its fears.

For the first time in many weary days.
    The child looked up, sweet smiling thro'
      her tears;
And when the nun the orphan bore within
    Where low, soft music fell upon their ears;
From her blue orbs the tears were dried. each
    one,
As dew dissolves on flowers at break of sun.

Before a stately painting. fair and tall.
    Of angels clothed in robes of spotless white.

They paused : the nun in simple childish
     words
   Told of the mother : how in the bright
Glad land above. like one of these, a spirit
     mild,
She dwelt and each hour watched o'er her
     lone child.

Pleased was the maid, seeming to understand;
   And from that hour there came no grief ;
The yearning heart was comforted indeed.
   To those who saw the change, a firm belief
Fastened itself (for true 'twas wonderful)
That they beheld a mystic miracle.

Yet. ne'er again for her lost parent did the
     child
   Lament ; but o'er her white face did there
     steal
A pensiveness ; and o'er the blue, a sadness ;
   While in the trembling voice, they seemed
     to feel.
Who knew her grown a woman, that its trill
Came as a spirit-echo o'er waters still.

SONG.

O! MONY years hae sped alang.
  Upon their way. upon their way.
Sin' we for aye our fareweel said.
  Beside the Tay, beside the Tay ;
But tho' the years gang like the wind
  Tha' blaws sae free. tha' blaws sae free.
My only thoughts. my bonnie lass,
  Are still o' thee. are still o' thee.

O! mony lads. my bonnie lass.
  May come to woo, may come to woo.
An' he wha wooes thee weel, I know,
  Will fin' thee true. will fin' thee true ;
Then lassie. think o' tha' fareweel
  At close o' day. at close o' day.
Think o' our last—our sad fareweel
  Beside the Tay, beside the Tay.

Altho' I ne'er thro' Scotia dear.
  Again maun roam, again maun roam.
In dreams my fancies fly to thee.

My dear auld home. my dear auld home.
An' ilka prayer I breathe at een.
   Sha' be for thee, sha' be for thee,
My bonnie lass— my native lan'—
   Across the sea. across the sea.

O, DEATH-PALE MOON OF EARLY MORN!

O, DEATH-PALE moon of early morn!
In ruin hung low over flower-shorn Autumn
    fields!
Sad eyed seraph! Sweet Selene! Fairest
    child of bright Hyperion!
Of two pure sisters, thou art fairest, being
    pale; for when the crimson car of Eos
    springs
Full high above the lone, fern-tangled fens,
    and genii-haunted glades of eastern
    woods;
Star-crowned, bright clad in robes of rose and
    gold, and deep o'erlaid with sapphire-
    tinted broidery,
Who is there shall say: Eos, the roseate maid,
    is lovliest? when, turning, he beholds
Poised o'er the russet fields, thy still white
    face; brighter for the dark clouds
    clustered round:

Brighter for the trailed black drapery of
    shadow-spirits winging swiftly past?
Beholding thee midst all the witchery of a
    slow-dawning gray November morn?
Shall not his sad heart tremble and his eyes
    shed tears watching thy waning loveli-
    ness ;
Viewing thee in all thy regal modesty, before
    thy sister's glances,
Fast fade, O. death-pale moon of early morn !
And merge in meadows sere ?

TO * * * *

Ah me! it is a fair, sweet name—
    Did they foresee,
The bud a perfect flower would frame,
    Who christened thee ?
A flower, as yet, not fully blown,
    But lovelier each unfolding grace,
    Wherein, what pleasure 'tis to trace
The future's promise, plainly shown ;
    To dream of what the flower will be
    Born of a budded purity.

Of thee, should e'er we twain, by fate
    Drift far apart—
Afar into the proud world's great
    Unquiet mart ;
Of thee, shall memory oft retrace
    Bright thoughts ; and songs, where still
        shall cling
    A sweet melodious murmuring
Of old time tenderness and grace.
    I ask of thee : The truth revere,
    And deem my friendship lasting, as
        sincere.

TO MATTIE.

BRIGHT, O bright, may thy bridal eve be !
  Never a cloud in the sky,
Only the moon-beams, mingled with star-gleams
  Glancing adown from on high.
Only the evening breeze, fresh from the locust
      trees,
  Laden with perfume divine ;
To tangle thy tresses with loving caresses,
  And sing whilst it blesses—
    "Happiness thine."

Bright, O bright, may thy bridal eve be !
  Happy the friends that are near.
Never a sadness, all joy and gladness,
  Never a sigh or a tear.

May the angels above surround thee with love,
 Guard thee and sit by thy side :
Music, and smiles, and flowers, from earth's
  fairest bowers,
 For the one no longer ours—
  " Mattie a bride."

Bright, O bright, may thy bridal eve be !
 Brighter the future before—
May the river of Time roll a rippling rhyme
 As thy bark drifts down its shore.
Come never a shock from reef or from rock,
 Come never a storm-cloud dark;
But the silver spray from the wavelet gay—
 May it ever play
  Before thy bark.

Bright, O bright, may thy bridal eve be !
 June roses are bursting bud.
The peonies blush red and the cherries o'er
  head—
 (Great tears of luscious red blood—)
Almost glow 'mid the green in the moon's
  yellow sheen.
 " Mattie"—I whisper it light :

As it falls in the cup where the honey bees sup,
 Each flower takes it up—
  "Mattie, good night!"

June, 1884.

L'ENVOY.

In Memoriam.—Obiit, Jan. 1885.

BRIGHT, O bright, may thy bridal morn be!

Swing open, O portals of Paradise! that I
 may behold her,

Clad as a bride, at the throne of the Mighty
 Redeemer.

Where time gives not pain, and the bride is
 the bride, though the ages wax older
 and older.

Where the ties torn asunder on earth are
 united;

And the mystery of life is dissolved, nor seen
 thro' the eyes of a dreamer.

CHASTELARD.

WARM breath, and lips, and cheeks deep,
    flushed with love ;
  Into the Queen's still chamber did he steal,
  Seeming the drowsy perfumed air to feel
Strike on his heart, fast beating, as a dove
Feeleth on pinion strong the airs above ;
  And, hid within the purple curtain fold,
Stood statue-wise ; nor once essayed to move ;
  So still. his very breath seemed stayed and
    cold.

Lo! but rest thou, mad pulse, the Queen is here!
  Before the crystal mirror sheen, a face ;
A clasp unloosed—a brooch withdrawn—a clear
  Soft throat, a luxury for eyes to trace——

Ha! One bold step. The Queen's heart beateth
    hard ;
And thou hast met thy death, Duke Chastel-
    ard !

LINES.

ON THE DEATH OF A CLASSMATE.

There's a vacant desk in the school-room now,
  There's a face we shall see no more;
There's a chill of death on a noble brow,
  There's a heart whose beatings are o'er.

There's a strand that is lost from a golden skein
  That affection and love have spun ;
There's a mystic thread that is snapped in twain
  That bound the hearts of a class as one.

But, O Harry ! when we gather again
  As with thee in the days gone by,
There'll be hearts that will ache with sadness
      then.
  There'll be tears in many an eye.

O ! our hearts go out with affection strong
  To that family bereft and sad ;
For the days to them will be drear and long.
  And their home in sorrow be clad.

Yet, when we think of the long weary way
  That thy feet on earth would have trod,
The gloom in our hearts is lit up with a ray,
  As we think of the angels, and God.

We can fancy we see them gathered around
  The form of a youth bright and fair ;
We can hear every joyful voice resound
  In an anthem, rich and rare.

We can fancy we see them place on his brow,
  Not the crown we had thought to place ;
Not the slender twig from the laurel bough,
  But the Christian's crown of grace.

SONG.

Away, away, ah me ! so far away ;
My soul's a-weary waiting day by day.
    O Time ! thy crutches fling.
    Trim as of yore thy wing,
Breathe thy soft breath o'er me and bear me
      home.
My childhood home so far, so far away;
Away, away, ah me ! so far away.
    So far, so far away.

Away, away, ah me ! so far away ;
The briar-rose, the alder bloom is gay.
    Green wheat has turned to gold.
    The harvest moon is bold.
Though all's so fair my heart is with my love ;
Is with my love so far, so far away.
My love, my love, so far, so far away,
    So far, so far away.

A VISION OF BOYHOOD.

GRADUATION POEM.

NOVEMBER winds are bleak and wild,
  November skies are gray ;
With leaden clouds the west is piled,
And the shades the morning sun exiled,
  Soon, soon will hold their sway.
Within the cottage, on the hearth
  The fire-gleams dance and play ;
And the little clock on the mantle-piece
  Says, tick—tick - tick. with a sound so gay
That the cricket crawls out from a chink
And stretches its wing with a wink and a blink
  And sings of the lost summer day.

      The door swings on its hinges
      And an old man passes out --
      Out into the gathering gloom
      Like a ghost from out a tomb ;
      Into the biting air, into the falling snow.
      With a weary tread and slow,
        He takes his way.

The falling flakes he heeds them not.
  Nor the wind so wild and high ;
He would wander away to some quiet spot,
And lay him adown and be forgot,
  And sleep while the years go by.
For he was only an old. old man,
  Too old for the world was he,
Little it cared for his sad, sad lot ;
Little it cared for the pleasure he got ;
  Never once did it look to see
    The tear-drop in his eye.

Slowly and sadly he wandered on
  Thro' flowerless meadows all still and white;
Up a wayside lane all dark and lone ;
  And into a wood where no gleam of light
Fell aslant the narrow winding way.
  There in the inky shades he lost himself :
Wandered hither and thither in dismay,
  Praying that some gentle woodland elf
    Might cross his path and lead him on
      aright.

Even as he prayed his prayer seemed answered.
Off to the right he seemed to hear,

Born on the blast that swayed the boughs
   o'er-head ;
Gentle, mellow, soothing, soft and clear,
   The purling of a tiny brook. And, led
By its sweet music, soon he stood
   Upon its bank, where swiftly on it sped
Along the border of the gloomy wood.

The great white moon rolled up the sky,
   And silvered the meadow across the rill ;
And burnished the tree tops swaying high,
   Till the wind blew off and the world grew
      still ;
And naught was heard save the lonely cry
   Of the owl on the distant hill.

Was it a flower the old man saw
   Across the stream in the gleaming snow ?
Was it a flower the driving flaw
   Blew down from the sky to bud and grow ?
He rubbed his eyes and he looked again :
   Ah ! strange such things should come to
      pass !
So he leaped across : O, mortal ken !
   He was up to his knees in waving grass !

Up to his knees in emerald green,
  Fragrant and fresh in a crystal dew ;
And the wonderful flowers that grew between!
  Crimson, scarlet, yellow and blue.
No wonder the old man grew perplexed,
  (Though the wonders had just begun)
He gazed on the moon, and lo! it waxed
  Full red in a gorgeous, glowing sun.
And the song of birds, and the hum of bees,
  And lowing cattle, and murmuring wind ;
And squirrel barks in the whispering trees
  That skirted the meadow not far behind ;
Made a mingled melody so wondrous rare
  That he stood and lifted his faded eyes,
And gazed and gazed thro' the realms of air.
  For he thought it came from Paradise.

I must away, at length he said,
I've lingered by this spot too long ;
Some faery band keeps overhead ;
Their spell is sweet, but ah, too strong.
I must away nor linger here,
Such charms can never last ;
They are too bright, too fondly dear ;
I must away, they hold me fast.

He wanders on, but no, the summer sun,
   The same that rose to him a moon,
Climbs up the sky. The squirrels run
   Across his path, and loud and sweet the tune
That flows from trembling bird-throats,
   Falls upon his ear. A path leads thro' a wood;
A wave of song along its border floats
   And bathes the blossoms in its mellow flood:
He follows down, his heart grows strangely
       light;
   A daring striped squirrel comes so near
To daunt pursuit, O wondrous sight!
   He gives it chase with one poor feeble cheer.

   Like Dr. Holmes' famous bay,
   "The same that drew the one-horse shay."
   That limbered up and won the race
   At such a mad, tremendous pace;
   The old man's limbs so supple grew
   They seemed almost as good as new.
   The squirrel soon, most scared to death,
   Mounted a tree to catch its breath.

Not pausing once to calmly stop and think
   He up and after; 'twas not so great a feat,

Though most all men as aged, I'm sure would
    shrink,
  Nor trust a branch to their poor trembling
    feet.
The squirrel safe from harm, he clambered
    down ;
  He felt so very queer he looked about and
    found
His shoes, and coat, and hat--that is the crown--
  Were gone ; gray hair and beard nowhere
    around :
All was changed ; he was a boy again, as glad
    and gay
  As any robin, wren or jay that ever flew.

Adown a road he kicked the dust before ;
Over a stile, and he stood once more
With a happy group by the school-room door.
When the bell o'erhead chimed out its lay,
With a lifted shout he left his play,
And with pitter-patter of naked feet
Filed into the room and took his seat.
There was the master with visage grave.
Stern was his voice, but manly and brave ;
There were the maps, and charts, and all,
The black-board stretching from wall to wall ;

And there was one—O Cupid's dart!
What feats ye work!   What spells impart!
Were ever sunbeams twined in curls,
Or teeth wrought out of snowy pearls?
O Life! no pleasure in thy jeweled cup
Is half so sweet as that we sup
When First-love lightly steals behind,
Clasping our eyes, declares us blind.

When school is out, and the twilight sweet
Comes stealing along o'er the emerald wheat;
With dinner pail swung on his arm,
He crosses the fields to his father's farm,
Gayly whistling his roundelay,
Cuts thro' the orchard—the nearest way;
Over the barn-lot fence he leaps—
The odor of supper hastens his steps:
He stands again in the open door—
His steps resound on the oaken floor—
A mother's kiss, O happy boy!
Thy bliss knows not the word alloy.
A father's, a brother's, a sister's love,
Radiant lusters from light above.

The evening meal is o'er at last,
The shadows are falling thick and fast,

The stars gleam out in the sky o'erhead,
The school-boy hies him away to bed ;
Softly sinks into sweet repose,
A rest that only childhood knows.

*   *   *   *   *   *   *

The last red coal upon the hearth grew black ;
The cricket ceased its lay; the clock ticked on;
The wind blew down the chimney with a moan.
And drifted the ashes gray about the feet
Of an old man sitting silently alone.
A tear-drop trickled adown his wasted cheek,
And falling upon his shrivelled hand
Roused him from his reverie.   Cease your
          shriek,
O wind !   He speaks : 'Twas but a sweet,
          sweet dream, he says;
Often they come, but too, too soon they fly;
On earth those days to me can never come.
O, that I could live them o'er again
Some where beyond the sky !

IN CAP AND BELLS.

In cap and bells the gay Fool came
Unto the court in search of fame ;
  In search of homage, not of bread,
  Nor gold. nor wit, but fame instead—
Most gold is dross, most wit is lame.

He got great praise of every dame ;
Of king. and court, in wealth aflame ;
  And honors swept the empty head
             In cap and bells.

Before the gates. with palsied frame,
A Sage, for alms, did ask in shame ;
  On stares, and sneers, and oaths he fed.
  Unto the Sage the gay Fool said :
For wealth and fame, a bawble aim.
             In cap and bells.

A CLASS SONG.

We are sailing, sailing away,
  Away from Youth's sunny land ;
Away from the spring-tide of life,
  With its blossoms so rare and grand.
Out. out from the silver-lined shore,
  Gently we drift with the tide ;
Farewell. ye bright days of the past!
  Farewell ! Let us sing as we glide.

      Sailing away, sailing away,
        Out on the ocean of life,
      Sailing away, sailing away,
        Hearts growing strong for the strife.
      Forever and ever farewell,
        School days so tender and rare,
      Farewell, farewell to you all,
        Life has naught else half so fair.

We are sailing, sailing away,
  And the shore will fade ere long
Like the days of the happy past ;
  For the wind of Time is strong,

And he bears Life's bark with a speed
   Thro' the waves that surge and break.
Whilst he leaves us naught but memory.
   Behind in the foaming wake.

We are sailing, sailing away.
   Never again shall we view
The sun-litten land of our youth,
   With its skies of purple and blue.
Yet we hope when the storms are o'er.
   And the end of our voyage nigh.
To harbor at rest from all care.
   By the jasper throne on high.

SONNET.

TO ——.

WHEN thieving Time, who steals away the
   bloom
  And sweets of life, upon his hurried way
  Comes stealing silently around thee, may
He linger long ere he essays to doom
Thy loveliness ; but back into the gloom
  And shadow of the Past hasten afar.
So, when Azrael, the white-robed, shall plume
  His noiseless wings for flight and come to
   mar ;
No time-worn, withered stalk, leafless and lone
  His icy breath shall meet ; but a rich flower,
Rare as the eastern sky at dawn, full blown,
  Blushing in its own beauty hour by hour.
A beauty with which all sweet ways combine—
Combine for painter's brush and poet's line.

OUR DEAD CHIEFTAIN.

AMONG the summer blossoms our gallant
    chieftain lay,
The lillies and the roses upon his lifeless
    clay.

We draped our banners o'er him, we laid his
    sword at rest
Where the lillies and the roses lay bright
    upon his breast.

Across the bier the soft wind blew, fresh from
    the summer sea ;
It kissed his face nor deigned to heed the
    sentry pacing silently.

It kissed his face and closed eyes, once lit
    with noble fire—
Fair eyes that flashed on treachery with patri-
    otic ire.

And the summer wind blew o'er the world,
    and on the hearts of men

There fell a sound of weeping too deep for
    mortal ken.

A wail and lamentation, fraught with a mighty
    grief,
The bursting of a Nation's heart beside her
    fallen chief.

No more for him the maddened charge—the
    clash of blood-stained arms ;
No more for him the sounds of strife and red
    war's wild alarms.

Among the summer blossoms he lay as one
    asleep ;
A mighty host came sadly up to view his face
    and weep.

Slow to the muffled drum-beat we followed
    where they led ;
Far from the tomb beside the sea was heard
    that solemn tread.

And we laid him softly, softly, to sleep the
    sleep of years
Among the summer blossoms wet with a
    Nation's tears.

ALAS, IT RAINS!

Alas, it rains! Through all the night
The cold drops fall, a bitter blight,
    Into the dead day's face, as fall
    Salt tears on shroud, and bier, and pall
Of some sweet singer, cold and white.

The embers gray throw a gray light
Upon the hearth ; my soul, in fright,
    Sighs: Dead is love, and hope, and all.
                Alas, it rains !

Yet, sitting there, I heard the flight,
Thro' the rude storm of angels bright,
    Meseemed to hear a low voice call :
    There is no rain past Heaven's wall ;
Fear not ; nor those sad words unite :
                Alas, it rains !

SYMPATHY.

MYSTERIOUS harp. wrought of pearl and gold !
  Clasped in fair Psyche's arms and gently
      pressed
  Close to her milk-white, gently throbbing
      breast.
What music doth thy trembling strings unfold !
Not loudly swelling. madly. fiercely rolled ;
  But gentle as the evening April wind
That sighs o'er beds of yellow cowslips bold,
  And nodding blue-bells, lovingly entwined.

A sigh. an old man's grief, a maiden's tear.
  An orphan babe, a wounded mother-bird ;
A child's distress o'er broken plaything dear,
  A beggar trembling 'neath some scathing
      word ;
All these thy strings of silver gently shake,
To such. what other harp is there can wake ?

THE KILLDEE.

Killdee, killdee, dee, dee ;
Over the fallow lea
      I hear thee call.
Dark is the April sky ;
Wild is the wind, and high ;
Yet thy shrill note hear I,
      Above it all.

Dee, dee, killdee, killdee,
No leaf on shrub or tree
      Can there be seen.
Yet, willow buds are white ;
Wind-flowers spring up by night ;
Pure snow-drop breasts are bright ;
      The meadows green.

Killdee, killdee, killdee,
Thy cry so wild and free
      Follows the blast.
At thy inspiring call,
Answer the green frogs all,
In notes that sweetly fall
      From o'er the waste.

Killdee, dee, dee, dee, dee.
No bird thou seemst to me
   Of earth's demand :
But some sad, lonely sprite ;
Lost in the dark of night
Whilst winging thy swift flight
   Toward faery-land.

Dee, dee, dee, dee, killdee,
A flash — right merrily
   The sun gleams out :
Before his cheering ray,
Swift hies the storm away,
Gloom hath nowhere to stay.
   Care's put to rout.

Dee, dee, killdee, dee, dee,
No sooner dost thou see
   The sun's bright beam,
When up into the blue
Thou cleavest the thin air thro',
Till falls the evening dew
   O'er meadows green.

Dee, dee, dee, dee, dee, dee,
Once more the fallow lea
   Holds thy white breast.

The twilight shadows fall ;
Again I hear thee call
From out the grasses tall
      That hold thy nest.

Killdee, though faint, yet clear,
Upon the breeze I hear
      Thy last good night.
Sweet bird, if ever dreams
Court thee, to me it seems,
Needs must they be bright beams
      Of heavenly light.

THE GHOST.

I MET a ghost upon the stair.   Said I:
　　Whence? Whither, O thou Ghost? The
　　　　shade replied:
　　From Heaven am I, and from the fountain
　　　　side
Where groweth the mystic Tree, mountain
　　　　high,
Of whose twelve fruits is TRUTH, that cannot
　　　　die.
　　Why stayest thou my steps, O, ghost of
　　　　Heaven?
Thou mortal, hear: Against high Heaven's
　　　　sky
　　TRUTH is graven in gold and white, and
　　　　given
Homage of God, and of all angels praise
　　Next after CHARITY.   TRUTH is a flower

Unbeknown to many ; he that dare raise
    Her banners, battles many a weary hour.

Seize thou her battered shield—her broken
        lance—
Lift high the shout, and hasten to advance.

www.ingramcontent.com/pod-product-compliance
Lightning Source LLC
Chambersburg PA
CBHW030018030726
47499CB00008B/3046